My Friend's a Gris-Kwok

Malorie Blackman

Illustrated by
Andy Rowland

Barrington  Stoke

First published in 2022 in Great Britain by
Barrington Stoke Ltd
18 Walker Street, Edinburgh, EH3 7LP

www.barringtonstoke.co.uk

This story was first published in a different form as
My Friend's a Gris-Quok (Scholastic, 1994)

This edition based on *My Friend's a Gris-Kwok*
(Barrington Stoke, 2013)

Text © 2013 & 2022 Oneta Malorie Blackman
Illustrations © 2013 Andy Rowland

The moral right of Oneta Malorie Blackman and
Andy Rowland to be identified as the author and illustrator
of this work has been asserted in accordance with the
Copyright, Designs and Patents Act, 1988

A CIP catalogue record for this book is available
from the British Library upon request

ISBN: 978-1-80090-162-9

Printed by Hussar Books, Poland

For Neil and Lizzy,
with love as always

CONTENTS

CHAPTER 1
How it Began

My best friend Alex is a Gris-Kwok!

What's a Gris-Kwok? you're thinking. Well, I didn't know either. But then I found out Alex's secret. And this is how it happened …

Early one Saturday morning, I popped over to Alex's house. Just as I rang his doorbell, a drop of rain splashed on my cheek. I looked up at the grey sky, and then I saw someone at the bedroom window.

It was Alex's awful little sister, Polly!

Alex opened the front door. "Hi, Mike!" he said with a grin. "Come in. Mum's out, so we've got the house to ourselves."

"I thought Polly's bedroom was at the back of the house?" I said.

"It is," Alex said. "Why?"

"Well, I just saw her in the front bedroom," I said. "She's making funny faces at me out the window." I pointed up at her. "Very funny faces."

"*What?*" Alex stepped outside to see what was going on.

I started to make faces back at Polly. I pulled my lips one way and my cheeks the other and screwed up my eyes.

"Mike, you're as bad as Polly. Come on." Alex grabbed my arm and dragged me into the

house. He kicked the door shut behind us and ran upstairs.

I didn't know what all the fuss was about, but I ran after him anyway. I soon found out. Alex went straight to his mum and dad's bedroom. He turned the door handle, but the door didn't open.

"She's ... she's locked the door!"

Alex was so annoyed. He bent to look through the keyhole and then stood up almost at once.

"Polly! Open this door right this *second!*" he yelled.

I could hear Polly laughing her head off inside the room. Alex began to hammer on the door.

"Polly, I'm warning you. If you don't come out, I'll tell Mum and Dad, and then you'll be in big trouble!" Alex bent to peep through the keyhole again.

"What's she doing?" I asked.

"Spraying Mum's posh perfume all over herself," Alex shouted.

I bit my lip to stop myself from laughing out loud.

"I should never have let her go upstairs on her own," Alex said. "Not for a moment. Mum warned me not to leave her by herself. But I was on the computer, and I wasn't really watching her."

"It's not your fault," I began. "You'll just have to—"

But Alex didn't listen. "*Polly!*" he shouted. "*Polly, don't you dare!*"

"What's the matter? What's she doing now?"
I asked.

"Rats! She's just turned herself into a bird,
and she's … Oops!" Alex slapped his hand over
his mouth as he turned to look at me. "Rats!
My mouth is bigger than the number 19 bus!"

I looked back at him.

"What did you say?" I asked. "Polly's turned
herself into a *what*?"

"A … a bird," Alex said. "A robin, I think.
And she's flying around the room."

CHAPTER 2

The Secret

I put my fingers into my ears and wiggled them about.

"I don't think my ears are working right," I said. "Did you just say Polly had turned into a bird?"

"She has. She's a robin," Alex said. He was looking through the keyhole again.

"Alex, I think that keyhole is doing something to your eyes – or your brain," I said.

Alex stood up and turned to me. "Mike, can you keep a secret?" he asked.

"Of course I can," I said. "What is it?"

"I'm going to tell you something," he said. "But you must promise that you'll *never* tell anyone else. Not even your mum and dad. And you must promise not to tell my mum and dad that I told you."

"I promise," I said right away.

"All right then," he said. "I think you'll understand better if I just show you. Hold on to my jumper."

"Why ...?"

"Don't ask questions," Alex said. "We don't have much time. We've got to get in there before it's too late. Polly's going to hurt herself. She doesn't know what she's doing."

"But we can't get in," I said. "The door's locked!"

"Grab hold of my jumper," Alex said.

I did what he told me.

"Ready?" he asked.

"Ready for what?"

"I'll explain later," he said. "Here we go!"

All of a sudden I began to feel very weird.
I felt squeezed and squashed and bunched up

and hunched up. My whole body tickled and prickled, my back most of all. I looked down, and then …

Oh no! Where were my feet? Where were my shoes? My legs had gone, and the carpet looked a long, long way down. It was like being in a plane and looking down at the land far below.

And where was Alex?

I looked around. I couldn't see Alex anywhere, but there was a fly right in front of me. A horrible, hairy, *enormous* fly! A whooshing sound filled the air. That was the sound of the fly's wings beating. Amazing!

And the hairy fly was heading straight for me!

"Zzzz!" I squeaked as I tried to get out of its way.

I was too slow. *Slap!* The fly hit me.

Then I felt as if I was falling, falling, falling to the ground. Bump! I looked down. I was kneeling on the floor, but my legs were back. So were my feet – and my shoes! I looked around, puzzled. Where had the big fly gone?

And more important, where was Alex?

Suddenly, Alex was in front of me again. It was so quick that I blinked to make sure my eyes were working. One moment Alex wasn't there; the next moment he was.

"Why did you smack into me?" Alex asked.
He had crossed his arms and was scowling
at me.

I got up as fast as I could. "What do you mean?" I asked. "There was this enormous fly coming straight for me, and it banged into me ..."

Alex was so annoyed his eyebrows almost joined up. "That was me, idiot," he said. "I was the fly!"

CHAPTER 3
Splinters Like Trees

I must have heard Alex wrong.

"Pardon?" I said.

"That was me," Alex said. "I turned into a fly. You turned into one too because you were holding on to my jumper when I changed."

"I turned into a fly?" I shook my head. "Oh, come off it, Alex!"

"It's true, I promise," Alex said. "You turned into a fly. You were flying and everything. But

I didn't have a chance to explain what I'd done before you banged into me. And then you came flying at me again and you changed back."

"Hang on a minute," I said. "I didn't fly at you. *You* bumped into *me*."

"Look, Mike, can we talk about which of us bumped into the other one another time?" Alex said. "Right now we have to catch Polly before she gets us all into big trouble. So hold on to my jumper while you change, then let go of me. When you've turned into a fly, don't touch me again until we've both flown through the keyhole. OK?"

I was too puzzled to argue, so I did as Alex said and took hold of his jumper.

He started to change, and so did I. The feeling of being squeezed and squashed and bunched up and hunched up came back, even stronger than before.

I looked down at my body. My arms and legs had turned into thin stalks covered in black hairs. My hands and feet had vanished, and I had things like claws instead. But the weirdest thing of all was the tickling, prickling feeling in my back.

At first it felt like something was scratching me on both sides of my back. Then it felt as if the skin on my back was being pulled and pinched. It didn't hurt. But there was something very odd going on.

Suddenly, I worked out what had happened.

Wings! I had wings! Yippee! They were wide and thin and very strong. I moved them together, then apart. I was flying. Wow!

"OK, Mike." Alex's voice was high and squeaky. "We're going to fly through the keyhole now," he said. "Stay close to me – but not too close – and be careful."

Alex flew towards the keyhole. I followed him. Whoosh! Whooosh! My wings beat the air.

"Mike! Don't get too close to me!" Alex called out.

I was so busy smiling at my wings that I had forgotten to look where I was going!

"Careful, Mike!" Alex warned me. "If you touch me when we're flying through the keyhole, you'll turn into a boy again, right in the middle of the door."

Ugh! That wasn't a very nice thought at all.

Alex flew right through the middle of the keyhole. I waited a second, then went after him. I looked around in surprise. All around me in the dark were huge pale trees with no leaves on them.

Then I saw that they weren't trees at all. They were *splinters*. I was so tiny that the splinters looked like the tallest trees in our local park!

"What's that stuff in the air?" I asked Alex.

"I'm not sure," he said. "I think it's dust. Our wings must be flicking up all the dust in the keyhole."

Wow! Who'd have thought that there could be so much dust in one keyhole? It was all around me now. My nose began to tingle, then to tickle, then to itch.

"Ahhhh … Ahhhh … Alex … I'm going …
to …"

"Don't sneeze, Mike," Alex said. "Please!
Hang on, or you'll crash into those splinter-tree
things."

"I … can't … help … it!" I gasped. "The dust
t-t-tickles m-my nose … aaa-aaa-aaa-aaa …"

Just then we reached the other side of the
keyhole. Everything was brighter and lighter.
Alex flew back near me.

"Hang on, Mike, I'll change you back," he called out.

"Aaa-aaa-aaa-aaa-choo!" I sneezed.

The power of the sneeze sent me flying backwards, and I smacked hard into Alex.

Blomp! We both landed on the ground with a thump.

I sneezed again: "Aaa-aaa-aaa-aaa-choo!" And again. "Aaa-aaa-aaa-aaa-choo!"

I got up and rubbed my itchy nose with one hand and my sore bum with the other.

"Mike, are you all right?" Alex asked.

I nodded.

"Good," he said. "Now we need to find my pesky sister. Polly ... Polly, where are you?" Alex walked into the middle of the room. "Come out right now, Polly! You just wait till I get my hands on you!"

I looked around. There was no one in the room apart from me and Alex.

"Where is she then?" I asked.

Alex shook his head. "She's changed into something else. She's only just learned how to change, so now she does it all the time. She's a real pain!"

"I still don't understand what's going on," I moaned.

I saw the key to the room was on a chair next to the door, so I picked it up and unlocked the door. At least that was one problem solved!

Alex looked under his mum and dad's bed.

"How come you and your sister can change into something else any time you want to?" I asked as Alex peeped around the side of the wardrobe. "Can you turn into chairs and planes and chewing gum and things like that?"

"Polly and I are Gris-Kwoks," Alex said. "Well, we're half Gris-Kwok. You see, Mum's a Gris-Kwok, but Dad is just a normal human."

Alex lifted up the duvet and peered under the bed again.

"We can't change into furniture or stuff like that," he told me. "We can only change into animals, birds, insects or fish, and we can only do it three times a day. Mum can change as often as she likes, because she's not half human like me or Polly."

"You look normal," I said.

"Yeah, I know," Alex said with a glum face. "It's sad, isn't it?"

"Mind you, your mum looks normal too," I pointed out.

"Yeah, I know," Alex said. He looked even more glum. "It's a shame, really."

"A Gris-Kwok though!" I said. "I've never heard of one of those before. Wow, you are lucky. I wish I could turn into something else whenever I wanted to."

"It was more fun before we all had to start chasing Polly around the house," Alex sniffed.

"You don't think she's done what we did and flown through the keyhole?" I asked.

I opened the door to see if Polly was out on the landing somewhere.

"No, Mike! Don't open the door ..."

Too late! A small brown mouse jumped up out of nowhere and ran straight for my feet. It stood in front of me and squeaked up at me.

Then I really made a fool of myself.

"Arrggghhh! A mouse!" I ran and jumped up onto a chair.

"Shut the door!" Alex yelled.

He dived across the bed and ran to the door to slam it shut. But he was too late. The mouse ran out onto the landing and down the stairs.

"Rats! Rats! Rats!" Alex said. "We've lost her."

"Was that Polly?" I asked. I was still feeling sick from seeing the mouse at my feet. I hate mice.

"Of course! Who else could it be?" said Alex. "Come on, Mike. I've got a plan. I know how we can catch Polly for sure."

CHAPTER 4

Scaredy Cat

"Hold on to my jumper again," Alex said.

I grabbed hold. "So what are we going to be this time?" I asked. I was looking forward to it!

Alex didn't say a word, but I felt my body change again. I was shrinking, shrinking, shrinking.

I fell on my hands and knees on the carpet. Then, as I watched, my hands began to change. Thick brown hair started to grow out of my skin. My ears were twitching too, as if they

were changing shape. Whiskers popped out
from under my nose, and the bottom of my back
began to tingle. *Whish!* I had a tail!

"I'm a cat!" I said.

I looked down at my paws. They were covered with sleek brown fur. Just then I felt like I wanted to lick them. It was an odd feeling!

"Come on, Mike. My sister's getting away," Alex said.

We dashed down the stairs. But when I was halfway down, I stopped.

I bent my legs, then jumped up onto the handrail. Easy! I looked down at the carpet. Then I jumped down, all the way into the hall. Double easy!

"Stop showing off, Mike," Alex said. "We've got to find Polly. You take the living room, and I'll look in the kitchen."

I ran into the living room and stopped just inside the door. I sniffed the air with my cat nose, then sniffed again.

"Alex, she's in here," I called out. "There's a strong smell of mouse."

Alex ran in. "Are you sure?"

"Positive." I nodded my head. "She's in here somewhere."

"Right! You stay by the door, and I'll track her down," Alex said.

He ran behind the sofa to search for his sister. I marched up and down in front of the door.

"Squeak!" I looked round and saw Polly running towards me.

"Oh no you don't, Polly," I called out. "No way are you going to get past me again."

Now that I was a cat, I wasn't afraid of a little mouse!

I would have got her if she hadn't played a dirty, mean trick.

I was just about to jump on Polly the mouse when Polly the mouse vanished!

In her place was Polly the elephant!

Every last bit of fur on my body stood up on end and my tail fluffed out – I knew that a cat was no match for an elephant.

I was just about to make a dash for it when Alex skidded out from behind the sofa and banged right into me.

And *boof!* Just like that, we were boys again, with a great big elephant in front of us.

CHAPTER 5
Stuck

"Polly, change back right this second!" Alex ordered.

Polly lifted her trunk and made a noise like a trumpet.

"Shhh!" Alex begged. "Or someone will hear you."

Polly lifted her trunk again and made an even louder noise than before!

"What's she's saying?" I whispered.

Alex shook his head. "I haven't a clue," he said. "I've never been an elephant, so I don't speak elephant language!"

Polly walked over to the sofa, turned round and sat down! Have you ever seen an elephant on a sofa? It's a very odd sight!

The sofa creaked and groaned – an elephant is much too heavy to sit on a sofa. I held my breath as I waited for it to collapse.

Alex rushed forward and jumped up next to Polly. He pushed against her big grey back to try to get her to stand up.

"Polly, *move!*" Alex puffed. "If you b-break this sofa, I'm the one who'll g-get into trouble, not you."

He looked at me. "Mike, don't just stand there. Come and help me."

I took a careful step onto the sofa. I'd never been so close to an elephant in my life. The fact that the elephant was Alex's little sister didn't make her any less scary.

The creaks and groans of the sofa were really loud now. I reckoned that it was going to explode into bits of wood and fabric all around us at any moment.

Alex and I pushed and heaved at Polly the elephant, but she would not move.

"When I count to three, really *push*," Alex gasped as we leaned against Polly. "OK. One! Two ..."

I was busy listening for Alex to say "three", which was my big mistake. Just after he said "two", Polly stood up and moved away while Alex and I were still leaning against her. We grabbed each other and tried to keep from falling, but ... *CRASH!*

We both fell off the sofa and onto the ground!

I bashed both my knees and got a mouth full of carpet fluff. It's hard to say who was more annoyed – me or Alex. Polly was really getting on my nerves now.

"Polly! Polly, put that down!" Alex rushed over to his sister, who had just picked up the fruit bowl off the dining table with her trunk.

Alex tried to get the bowl away from her, but Polly waved her trunk in the air above his head.

I went over to help. We jumped up and down, up and down, but Polly's trunk was too high above us.

"Polly, don't drop that or you'll smash it!" Alex ordered. "Give it to me."

Polly did as Alex said. She gave it to him all right! She tipped all the fruit in the bowl on his head.

"Oww!" While Alex rubbed his sore head, Polly started to do something that made me back away from her.

"Alex ..." I began.

Polly was sucking up lots of peanuts from a dish on the table with her trunk. I had a horrible feeling ... and I was right!

Polly started to fire the peanuts at her brother and me. They smacked! They stung! They smarted! They *hurt*! I ran for cover, with Alex close behind me.

"I came round for some fun, not to be shot at with peanuts!" I moaned.

Alex and I popped our heads up from behind the armchair. Polly started to trot towards us.

"Don't take another step," Alex commanded. But Polly just ignored him.

"Why don't you change us into something else?" I said to Alex. "Change us into mice. I read somewhere that elephants are scared of mice."

"I can't," Alex said. "I can only change three times a day, and I've used them all up."

"But you were only a fly and a cat," I said. "That's two."

"No, I was a fly *two times*," Alex said. "Remember?"

"So what are we going to do?" I asked.

Polly the elephant was only a few steps away from us now. We backed away out of the room as she came closer and closer.

"Polly, I'm warning you ..." But Alex didn't finish what he was going to say.

By now we were out in the hall, and Polly was still trotting towards us. She was halfway through the door when it happened!

She got stuck! Well and truly stuck.

She wiggled and jiggled, but she couldn't move backwards, forwards or sideways.

"Serves you right, Polly," Alex said.

"Yeah! A double dose of serves you right with toffee sauce on top!" I added.

Just at that moment, we heard a key in the front door.

"Mum! Mum's back!" Alex panicked.

But just as the door opened, Polly changed back into her "normal" self. Alex scooped her up into his arms.

"Hi, Mum," he panted.

"Hello, Mummy!" Polly said. She stuck her thumb in her mouth and began to suck on it.

I couldn't believe it. She looked like a little angel in Alex's arms – as if she'd never do anything even a little bit naughty.

"Hello, everyone!" Alex's mum smiled. "Alex, has Polly been good?"

"She hasn't been any trouble at all, has she, Mike?" Alex said to me.

"No, Mrs Lessing," I said. "She's been really good." I crossed my fingers behind my back.

"Give her to me," Alex's mum said. "It's time for her nap."

"Happy to." Alex handed his sister over. "Let's go over to your house, Mike." Then he said, under his breath, "Come on before Mum explodes when she sees all the fruit and peanuts on the carpet."

"My house will be boring after all this," I said as Alex's mum went upstairs with Polly.

"That's why I want to go over there," said Alex. "If your roof is hit by lightning and wild horses run into your kitchen, it will still be more relaxing than this place!"

And you know something? He was right!